We Played Marbles

by TRES SEYMOUR

illustrated by DAN ANDREASEN

Orchard Books · New York

Orchard Books, 95 Madison Avenue, New York, NY 10016

Manufactured in the United States of America
Printed by Barton Press, Inc. Bound by Horowitz/Rae
Book design by Mina Greenstein
The text of this book is set in 22 pt. Nicolas Cochin.
The illustrations are oil paintings reproduced in full color.
1 3 5 7 9 10 8 6 4 2

Library of Congress Cataloging-in-Publication Data
Seymour, Tres.
We played marbles / by Tres Seymour ; illustrated by Dan Andreasen.
p. cm.
Summary: When friends playing on a Civil War battlefield begin to imitate what happened there,
Papaw asks them to quit because he knows a better game.
ISBN 0-531-30074-9 (trade : alk. paper). – ISBN 0-531-33074-5 (lib. bdg. : alk. paper)
1. United States–History–Civil War, 1861–1865–Juvenile fiction.
[1. United States–History–Civil War, 1861–1865–Fiction.
2. War–Fiction. 3. Play–Fiction.] I. Andreasen, Dan, ill. II. Title.
PZ7.S5253We 1998 [E]–dc21 97-26876

For my grandfather, Bill Seymour
who preserved the Fort and its story
for all of us who came after.

—T.S.

For Amazing Sharon

—D.A.

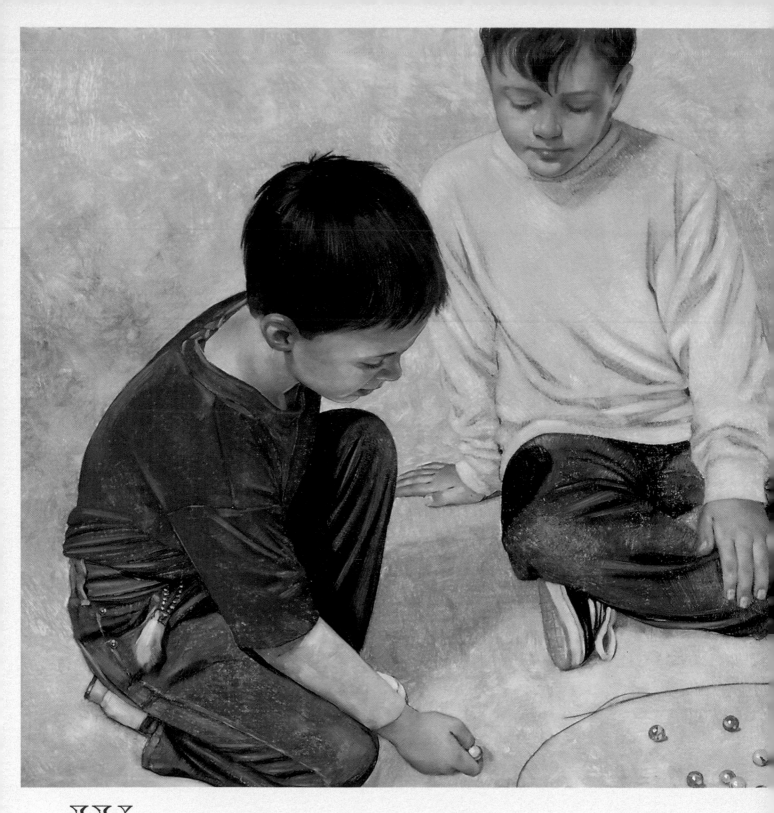

We played marbles on our Papaw's farm,
on the high dirt mounds of old Fort Craig
left over from the Civil War,

where hard, round Rebel bullets
used to pass Union bullets in the air.

We rode a pony (his name was Bob)
down the steep green banks of old Fort Craig,
where the cavalry came rushing
into barking guns

and Colonel Smith fell off his horse,
just like me.

We made mud pies on old Fort Craig,
salted with rocks and sweetened with hay,

where men in blue sat in the cold light
in the morning river fog
and ate a watchful, worried breakfast
of old biscuits and warm water.

We ran footraces on the long, slow slope
leading up to old Fort Craig
like the charge of Mississippi gray

that shouted Rebel yells to beat the band
until the guns shouted louder.

We chewed on grass stalks in the summer sun,
lying on our backs on old Fort Craig,

looking at the old Green River Bridge
our great-great-great-grandfather built
that caused all the fighting in the first place.

We threw a softball on the top of old Fort Craig,
and home base was the twisted, giant tree
a cannonball had smashed clear through.

Papaw says the cannon got left after the battle,
at the bottom of the pond.

We played soldiers,
shooting stick guns and
waving stick swords on old Fort Craig,
just like those people dressed in blue and gray

till Papaw came on out and said to quit.

He didn't say, "You'll hurt yourselves,"
like anybody else would say—

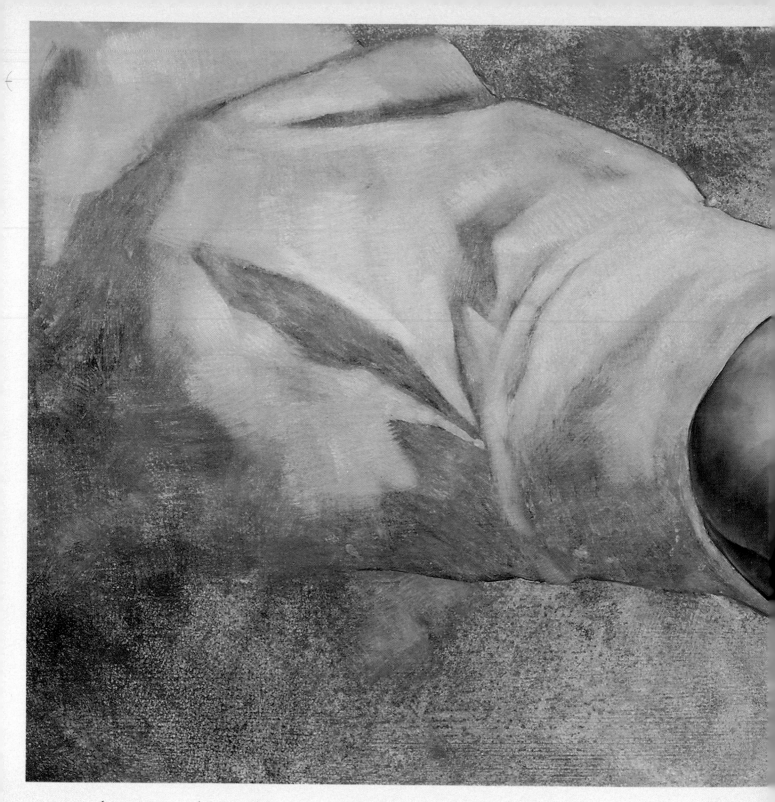

he just took an old, round bullet from his pocket,
and he said, "I know a better game."

So, we played marbles.

AUTHOR'S NOTE

In September 1862, a great battle of the
Civil War took place near Munfordville,
Kentucky, at Fort Craig. Four thousand Union
soldiers kept back an entire Confederate army for three
days, to protect the Green River Bridge, before
surrendering. Over three hundred people were hurt,
and some died. Fort Craig still stands, quiet and
peaceful now and covered with grass, on a farm
near Munfordville. Children have played marbles
there, using old bullets as shooters, for many years.